# THE
# LONELY
# BOOK

PRAISE FOR MEG GREHAN'S *BABY TEETH*

A *Kirkus* YA Book of the Year 2022
Shortlisted: An Post Irish Book Awards 2021
Nominated: Carnegie Medal 2023

"Emotionally rich and gloriously queer"
— *Kirkus,* starred review

"By turns realistically sweet and thorny"
— *Publishers Weekly*, starred review

"This enchanting work is an excellent addition to
LGBTQIA+ and verse novel collections."
— *School Library Journal*

"Skillfully charts uncertainty, temptation and
the course of a strange, desperate love."
— Imogen Russell Williams, *The Guardian*

PRAISE FOR MEG GREHAN'S *THE DEEPEST BREATH*

A *Bank Street* Best Children's Book of 2022
with Outstanding Merit

A *Booklist* 2021 Editor's Choice

Winner: Judge's Special Prize,
Children's Books Ireland Awards 2021

Shortlisted: Waterstones Children's Book Prize 2020

"Heartwarming and tear-provoking"
— *Booklist*, starred review

"Wholesome, powerful and essential"
— *Shelf Awareness*, starred review

"I spent most of this beautifully written verse novel blinking
back tears. ... I felt genuinely distraught to have finished it.
Amazing to think it's only Grehan's second book."
— Sarah Webb, *The Irish Independent*

# THE
# LONELY
# BOOK

## MEG GREHAN

Little
Island
Books create waves

THE LONELY BOOK

First published in 2023 by
Little Island Books
7 Kenilworth Park
Dublin 6W
Ireland

A British Library Cataloguing in Publication record for this book is
available from the British Library.

Cover illustration and chapter head illustrations by Nene Lonergan
Cover design by Anna Morrison
Typeset by Rosa Devine
Printed by CPI Group (UK) Ltd, Croydon CR0 4YY

Print ISBN: 978-1-915071-44-6
Ebook ISBN: 978-1-915071-41-5

Little Island has received funding to support this book from the Arts
Council of Ireland / An Chomhairle Ealaíon

10 9 8 7 6 5 4 3 2 1

for mum
growth and resilience and love love love
thank you
for everything

The best thing about summer
Is getting to hang out at the shop
At Birch Books
Mum
And Mama
And Charlotte
And me
Annie

The shop feels extra-magical in the morning
When we open the doors and the windows
And the sun streams in
And the books
Welcome us
And the smell of paper envelops us
And we get to work
Dusting or sorting or stacking
And Mum checks out the day's stack

How do I explain the stack?
Well
You see
Every single day
When we arrive at the bookshop
Right there
Sitting proud and excited
On the counter
Is a stack of books

Different books every day
Books about animals or witches or different worlds
About politics or geography or nature
And every day
We accept our magical mission
To find the books
Their owners
Their people
Their readers

My moms own the bookshop
They owned it even before I was born
Sometimes
They say it was their first
Baby
And we laugh

They named it Birch Books
Because they had their first kiss
Under a birch tree

They love the bookshop
All its dusty corners and
Wobbly shelves
Every stack of books
And every tinkle of the bell
Above the door

It's my home
My second home

And how lucky I am
To have two
Stacked right on
   top
   of
   each
   other

My sister
Loves the bookshop too
Of course she does
She especially loves
Helping people choose books
For people they love
I swear she knows
Every book in the
Whole shop
And she always
Knows the
Exact right
One
For everyone

My sister Charlotte
Is what you
Might call
        *Girly*
Though she hates that word
She likes dresses and long hair and glitter
She likes books about love and princesses

She is sixteen years old and very pretty
She is my sister
And I love her

Charlotte is always reading
She loves the shop
I think in her mind
It is our real home
And the apartment above
Is just where we sleep

She loves helping people pick out books
She loves talking about books
Sneaking them upstairs to read into the night
Organising them neatly
Displaying them prettily
She loves books
She loves our bookshop
She loves us
She loves us a lot
Just like we love her
My moms are very different
Mum is tall and thin and has hair down to her bum
She wears floaty skirts and long scarves
She likes thrillers and mysteries and books that
    make you leave the light on at night
She likes dark coffee and smelly cheese
She loves our Mama more than anything in the world
Except us

Except us
She loves us like a lion
Like a tiger
A dragon maybe
She loves
Ferociously

Mama
Is softer
She is squishier
She is shorter than Mum
And has hair that falls in neat curls to her shoulders
And the biggest best smile I think I've ever seen
She likes romance books and books set years and
    years ago
My Mama is always smiling
She glows
She has dark skin and kind eyes and
She loves gently
Warm hugs and kisses on the forehead
She loves
Gently

We are a family
Perfectly formed
We are made of love

Our bookshop
Is under our apartment

Just down the stairs
And it means the world to us
We spend all day there
Most days
Sorting and unboxing and recommending
Charlotte and I get to sit on the beanbags and read
Read anything we want
We must have read
Half the shop by now
We love it
It's part of our family

My moms opened the shop
When they were young
Only in their twenties!
Way before I was born
It's hard to imagine
Them so young
But I like to try
I like to think about them
Young and in love
Getting the keys for the first time
Holding hands as they walked through the door
Laughing together as they built shelves
And filled them with
All the best books

They are still like that
Holding hands

Laughing together
They are still full of love
For each other
For the shop
For us

The magic started
Around two years in
My Mama says
They started noticing
Books
Appearing on the counter
Out of nowhere
They would put them away
But they'd reappear just a minute later
They would ask each other
'Hey
Why did you put this here?'
But the other would swear that they didn't

Then the customers would arrive
Asking for a book
Just like the mysterious book on the counter
And it would happen
Again
And again
And
Again

Eventually
More and more books would appear
Every morning
A small stack would sit on the counter
Waiting eagerly
To be sold

Mum says
The shop wanted to help
And they accepted its help
Gratefully

The stack is big today
Eleven books
Sitting patiently
Waiting for their people

I pick up the first book
It's about snakes
I put it right back down
No thank you

I pick up the second book
It's a massive one
With a queen on the front
Crown on her head and sword in her hand

Before I can investigate the rest
Mama asks me to dust the children's section
The best section
And I go
Duster in hand
To visit my friends
To make sure they are dust-free and ready to find
    their homes

The snake man arrives before lunch
He has a tattoo of a snake
Wrapped around his forearm
So he's easy to spot

'Good morning'
I chirp
'This is for you!'
And I plop the book into his hands
He blinks
Then blinks again
'How did you—'
'Magic'
I say
But I don't think he believes me

I tell him I'm scared of snakes
While he's paying Mama
And he says there's no need to be
He says no snake has ever
Hurt him
And he trusts that they never will
And I nod and say
Maybe they just look scary
And he smiles and nods
And I decide to be a little braver

A woman arrives for the queen
In the early evening
She is small and shy
And hides her hands in her long jumper sleeves
Mama approaches her quietly and shows her the book
And her eyes light up
And she takes it and she clutches it to her chest
And she smiles

When she leaves I ask Mama how she knew the
    book was for her
And she says
She saw a gentle power
In the woman
A strength disguised as weakness
A power disguised as shyness

We start to close up the shop
In the evening
Tidying and counting and shelving

There's one book left to be collected
So we wait
Leaving the door open until the very last moment

'How strange'
Mama says
Looking at the very last book
Sitting alone on the counter
Waiting for its person
'How strange'
Says Mum

How strange
I think

This never happens

Every day
The stack appears
Before we arrive
The books sit on the counter
Waiting for us
And we thank the shop
And we feel it say
'You're welcome!'
And we spend the day
On the lookout
Waiting for the bell above the door to ring
And the perfect person to walk in
So we can unite them with their
Perfect book
And see them smile
And every day
At the end of the day
Every book in the stack is gone
Except today
Except
This book
Sitting alone and lonely on the counter
Unclaimed

'What do we do?'
I ask Mama
And she shrugs
I turn to Mum

And she shrugs too
I look at Charlotte
And she just looks at the floor

I look at the book
The last lonely book
With its yellow and purple cover
And a long title I can't quite make out
And I shrug too
And say
'Maybe tomorrow'
Half to my family
Half to the book
And we turn off all the lights
And we lock the door
And we go upstairs

At dinner we talk about all the books
We found homes for today
I tell Charlotte about the snake man
And Mama tells Mum about the queen woman
Charlotte tells us about a kid who squealed in
    excitement
Over a book about a magician
And his pet dragon
And Mum says she's still
So baffled
About the last book
And she wonders

Will it still be there in the morning
Or have we
Failed it?
And I cross my fingers under the table
And hope it will still be there
Waiting for us to try again

When the moms are tucking me in that night
They take turns kissing me on the forehead
And leave me to read by my night light
Until I fall asleep
And dream of snakes and queens and magicians
And a mysterious book
Just out of reach

The next morning
There is a new stack
And right on top
Is the book
Its cover
Purple and yellow
Standing out in the morning sun
Bright and glossy and demanding
'Find my person'
It seems to say
'Please'

Strange things happen throughout the day
The shelves seem to shiver

Books slide out and I spend all day
Pushing them back in
The revolving bookmark stand keeps spinning
And spinning and spinning
No matter how many times
I stop it

There's a weird energy in the shop
We all feel it
It isn't happy
The book sits like an omen
Lonely and solemn

The shop must be unhappy
I think
About the book sitting on the counter
Still
Seemingly
Unwanted

We all look at everyone who walks in with hope
Painted all over our faces
Please
We all seem to think
Please be the person
Please take the book
Please
Before the magic gets crankier
More restless

But all day
Very few people come in
Someone collects a cookbook
Someone collects a ghost story
No-one collects the lonely book
And by the end of the day
The shop's magic seems to crackle
Just a little
A little static
Buzzing in our ears
Tickling our fingertips
I'm worried
The shop will keep getting
More and more
Unhappy
I'm worried
About what that means
About what it might
Do

Mum scoops up the book
And plops it on one of the shelves
Behind her
And I wish I'd had a better look
When I had the chance

We talk about it at dinner
Mum seems sure it will stop
That someone will come for the book

She seems sure
But I'm not sure how real it is
Mama is concerned
She saw a book fall to the floor
All by itself
And it made her worry
Charlotte is quiet
But after a little while
She says
With such confidence
That I have to believe her
That she knows
She *knows knows knows*
That the book will be gone soon
That the shop will be OK
That the magic will settle
That we just have to give it time
That we're nearly there
Then she smiles at us
And I can't help but feel better
Though I have no idea
How she knows
How she seems so sure

The stack is small today
Smaller than usual
And Mum
Stares at it for a while
Then sighs
And starts looking through the books
Ignoring the lonely book
Right on top

'Some cool books today Annie!'
She exclaims
Flipping her long hair over her shoulder
'It'll be fun to find their readers!'
And she sounds happy
Chirpy
Even
So I choose to be happy too

Mum has been
A little
Different
Lately
A little more
Distracted
I suppose
Quiet

I don't know
If anyone else has
Noticed
But quiet knows quiet
And I see it
I've noticed

Charlotte
Is out all morning
And I miss her
I always love the shop
But it's best when
We're all
Here

I don't know
What she's up to today
But I hope she's having
A nice time
She's been so
Preoccupied
Recently

It's quiet today
In the shop
Someone buys a
Birthday gift
Someone buys
A travel guide

Mostly I read
I let myself sink into
A beanbag
And I read about a girl
Falling in love with
Another girl
It's so cute
And it makes me think
About my moms
I know they didn't have
Books like this when they were
My age
Mama always says that I'm
Lucky
To have the world in my hands
And she makes sure the
Shelves of our shop
Are full of all sorts of stories
That anyone who comes here
Can find themselves in
I decide to show Mum
The book I'm reading
I know she'd like it
I find her at the
Counter and

Mum doesn't know
I see her
Slide a book
Off the top of the stack

A big book
With euro signs all over it
She slides it off
And slips it into her bag
Under the counter
And I know
I know
It's wrong
But when she goes to help
Someone get a book off the
Highest shelf
I sneak a look
   I know
   I know

It's a book about money
   Finance
       Saving and saving and
               Saving
And something
Squirmy
In my middle
Worries that it's the shop
That needs saving
That maybe it's
Us

I can't imagine my family
Without the shop
Can't imagine the shop
Without us

I try to be happy
All day
The happiest ever
I try to help people pick books
I make new displays
I dust extra thoroughly
I sing little songs as I work and I
Hug my moms
Three times each

I try to fill the shop
With goodness
With lightness
With happiness

I help a person
Pick out five books
Five!
I listen to her very closely
And think about all the books I know
And together we find the perfect ones
And as she's paying at the counter

I watch Mum
To see if she looks happy
Relieved
But she just gives her usual kind smile
Then goes back to work

I'll have to try harder

Mama and I go do the food shop
In the afternoon
I like the supermarket
Something about it
Calms me
I like how everything has a place
And it never changes

I try to enjoy my time with my Mama
To have fun playing silly games
And talking about the swoony new book she's
    reading
And how we don't understand how Mum can read
About criminals and lies and deceit
Late at night
And not get scared
'She's very brave'
Mama says proudly

But I'm worrying about the shop
About the big book with the euro signs

So I ask her
'Hey, Mama'
'Yes, bug?'
'If we didn't have the shop
What would you want to do?'
And I cross my fingers behind my back
That she has lots of fun answers
That there are a million things she wants to do
That she could be happy elsewhere

'My goodness'
She says
Taking a big breath
Her curls bouncing
'I can't even imagine!'
I uncross my fingers
They didn't help

At home
We make dinner together
All of us in our tiny kitchen
We play music
And chop vegetables
And dance and laugh and bicker over
Too much salt or not enough salt
This song sucks and no it doesn't
We make lasagne and smother it with cheese
We see who can butter the garlic bread the fastest
We have fun

We are together
And the music is loud
And our laughs are louder
And everything is OK

While we're eating
Charlotte says the shop was quiet today
And she's glad she got to read
Almost all afternoon long
I look at Mum and Mama
They don't smile
But they ask her about the book she's reading
And she spends the rest of dinner
Telling us every detail
Of the plot so far

She tells us about princes and princesses and first
    kisses and first loves and lavish balls and gowns
    and castles
And we all listen
Enraptured
Because she speaks so passionately and it's nice
To see her
Bright and
Bubbly and
Charlotte

I go to sleep
Sure

So sure
That the book will find its home the next day
And I wake
Excited
But by noon
No-one has arrived

We really start to feel the changes

The shop starts to feel
Different
It has a new energy
Usually so calm and cosy and
Gentle
It seems suddenly anxious
Impatient
Wrong

All day
I can't stop worrying
About the mystery book
The lonely book
Of course
But mostly
About the book in Mum's bag
About the shop
About the future

What would happen if the shop closed
What would happen to the magic
To the books
To us?

I decide it's time to do something
I sit in a corner

Where the beanbags are
Hidden in the kids' section
And I think
And I think
And I think
And I come up with
Nothing
Nothing
Nothing

I get a notebook
And a pen
And I sit on the beaten-up
Squishy sofa
Near the history shelves
And I think
And I think
And I think
And I come up with
Nothing
Nothing
At all

I try the travel section
The young adult section
I try pacing
And wandering
And humming
I try

Just about
Everything
I can
Think of
But no ideas come

Just before closing
When there are only two books left on the
    counter
The mysterious lonely book
And a tome about necromancers and talking cats
    and magic
A woman appears
And says
'Hello
I am looking
For a book
A tome
Really
About necromancers
And talking cats
And magic'
And Mum smiles
And says
'Here you go!'
And hands her the book from the counter
And the woman gasps
And says
'Wow!

You must be magic!'
And Mum just laughs
And says
'What a coincidence!'
With a secret wink in my direction
And suddenly
I have an idea

I stay up late
Sitting on my bed with a notebook
My ideas swirling and twirling and dancing
   around my head
We need
I think
I am sure
We need
To share our magic
We need to let people know
We have magic
Our little shop
Is full of it
It's in every nook and cranny
Every book is steeped in it
Every page
Every word

Maybe
I think
If we let people know
About our magic
More people would come to the shop
Maybe the stack
Would get bigger and bigger
Every single day
Maybe even the owner of the mystery book

Would come
Maybe the shop
Would be happy again
And we
Would be
Too
Mum and Mama and Charlotte and me

I try to come up with ways to let people know
Ways to get the word out
But I'm sleepy
And it's late
And soon
My eyes are heavy
And soon
I'm asleep
And soon
I'm dreaming
About dragons and bookshops and mages and
    moms and Charlotte and me and
Magic magic magic

The next morning at breakfast
I try to bring up my idea
Mum is frying eggs
Mama is reading the paper
Charlotte is telling us the plot of her latest book
Reading out her favourite quotes
Swooning over the romance
I am thinking

Waiting
Wondering
Eventually
When Mum sits down with her eggs
I burst out
'I THINK WE SHOULD SHARE THE SHOP'S MAGIC'
It explodes from me
Everyone stops what they're doing
And looks at me
Forks clatter onto plates
The paper falls to the table
'What?'
Charlotte asks
'Why?'
Mum asks
'How?'
Mama asks
I take a deep breath
'I think it would help'
I say
'I think it would bring more people in'
I say
'I think it could'
   I want to say
   Save us
   But the words won't come out
Mum is looking at me funny
Like she knows what I'm thinking
She's looking at me so intently
I have to look away

'No'
Charlotte says
'No way'
I look at her
'Why?'
I ask
And it comes out small and weak and quiet
'No way'
She says again
Big and strong and loud
Our moms are looking at us
Back and forth between us
'It would be dangerous'
Charlotte says
'It would be great'
I say
I want to tell her about the book in Mum's bag
About the euro signs all over it
I want to tell her what it means
I want to tell her we're in trouble
I want to tell her this could save us
But I can't
I wouldn't
It isn't mine to tell
And anyway
I don't want to worry her
To scare her
'I just think'
I murmur
'That it would be good

We're so lucky'
I say
'So lucky to have this magic
I just think
I think we should
Share it'

I want to tell her
That it would help
That we deserve
More customers
The shop does
Our moms do
That people deserve
To know
To share in this gift
That it could change
Everything for us
That it could change
Everything for our moms
But my words won't come
They're so loud
In my head
So brave in my head
So strong
So sure
But once they hit my
Tongue
They fizzle
Out

'Well I say no'
Charlotte says
Standing up
Clutching her book to her chest
'No no no
We aren't *ready* for that'
And she storms out
And I'm so
Confused
I'm so
Hurt
I turn to my moms
And they look shocked
They look just as confused as I feel
'Will you think about it?'
I ask them
My voice still
So small
They look at each other
'I don't know if that's a good idea'
Mum tells me
And Mama nods quietly
'I think'
She says
'It's best kept
A secret
Just to be
Safe'
I nod
Though I don't feel like nodding at all

And I leave the table
Go to my room
Sit on my bed
And cry
Just a little

I'm so frustrated
I'm so mad
That my words got trapped
That I couldn't
Push them out
Especially with my family
Especially
When what I had to say
Was so
Important
So important
To me
So true

Sometimes
I just go
Quiet

My words get stuck
In my throat
My chest
My tummy
My head
I get full up

With everything I want to say
But it just won't
Come out

It was scary
The first few times
I would open my mouth
But nothing would come out
The words were there
Forming a lump in my throat
Choking me up
I cried
And cried
And Mum and Mama
Looked so
Scared
They tried to calm me
But it was Charlotte
Charlotte who got me to breathe
In and out
In and out
In      hold      out
In      hold      out
To write down what I wanted to say
Which helped
Helped me feel less
Trapped in myself
Less stuck
Less helpless

Eventually my speech came back
I woke in the morning
And said 'hi everyone'
Without even thinking
And Mama hugged me
And asked if I was OK
And I said 'yeah
I think so'
And Mum said
'Do you know what happened?'
And I said 'no
I just got
Quiet'

It happened again
A little while later
My words
Disappeared
We were in the supermarket
And Mum asked me to go get the stinky cheese
But when I went up to ask the man
Who was smiling very kindly at me
No words would come
I could think them
But I couldn't speak them
And I started to feel
So uncomfortable
So panicked
I tried

Really I tried
I spluttered and pushed and tried and tried and
    tried
Then I turned
And I ran

Mum took me to the doctor
The next day
And I explained what was happening
Mum let me use my own words to describe
What it was like for me
I wrote it all down and she read it for me
And it was weird
To hear my words
Without my
Voice
And the doctor looked at me with kind eyes
And she said it's something called
*Selective mutism*

She said sometimes
Usually if I'm uncomfortable
Or stressed
Or worried
My words
Might not come
She said not to be too scared
That they will come back

Mama asked what I needed
As she hugged me
When we got home
And I told her
I just need
To feel
Some type of
Control
To feel
That I'm not
All alone
In my
Silence

Charlotte suggested
Sign language
And the idea made me so happy
To be able to communicate
Even when I can't talk
Makes me feel
Safe
So we all started learning
We go to lessons together
On Wednesday evenings
And during the week we sit together on the couch
And practise
And it makes me feel
So loved
So important

So valued
Now
I wish I could
Understand
That's all I want
Really
Just to understand
Why Charlotte got so mad
Just to understand
Why our moms think we wouldn't be safe
If we shared our secret
Our wonderful secret
Our secret that does nothing but help us
Help other people
Help books find their readers
Readers find their books
What could be so wrong about sharing that joy?
What could be so bad?

Charlotte is off with me all day
The only time I see her smile is when she's
    helping a little boy pick out some books for his
    birthday
She finds him books about fairies and history and
    dinosaurs
And he looks so happy as he leaves with his dad
And Charlotte looks
So at peace
Then she meets my eye
And scowls

And I feel
Terrible
All over again
But I don't know
What I did
So wrong
And I want to ask
I want to talk to her
I want to talk to my sister
And figure out why what I said made her so mad
But when I move towards her
She spins on her heel
And stomps off to tidy the cookbooks

The day is long
The shop still feels off
The lonely book is still on the counter
The stack was smaller than usual today
Nothing feels quite
Right
Eventually though
It's time to go home
To go back upstairs
And eat and rest and get ready
To try again tomorrow

Dinner is tense
Mum and Mama try their best
Chatting and joking and laughing
But Charlotte is still mad at me

And I'm still sad about it
Charlotte and I never fight
She might be older than me
But she never makes me feel
Smaller
We are friends and sisters and we love each
other
But today
Today it doesn't feel that way
Not even a little
Today it feels like she wants me to go away
And I don't know what to do

I try to decide if I should bring up the magic
again
Or if that would make everything worse
I know if I could just be brave and confident
I could convince them
If I could just
Say everything on my mind
But I know once everyone's eyes are on me
I'll get shy again
Like this morning
When the words were on the tip of my tongue
But just
Wouldn't
Come out

I don't know why I get shy
I trust my family

I know they'd never make fun of me
Or make me feel stupid
But sometimes
My words just get stuck

Dinner passes by
And afterwards
Charlotte goes straight to her room
And music seeps out from under the door
The surest sign
She doesn't want company

'Mum'
I say
As she's washing the dishes
And I'm drying
Both of us somehow
Covered in suds
'Where do you think the magic comes from?'
She stops for a second to think
'You know
I'm not so sure'
She says
'But sometimes
I think it
Comes from
Us'
And I like that idea
I like it a lot
'I think maybe

We poured so much love and happiness and hope
Into it
We mixed it into the paint we put on the walls
The wood we built the shelves with
Into every book we chose to fill them with
And I think it knew
It felt it
And it wanted to show us love too
So it does
Every day'

And it makes me think
About how
Unhappy
The shop is right now
How sad it seems to feel
About that one little book
And it makes me think
That maybe it's not just any book
And maybe
It's not just for any person
But someone it sees as
Important
Someone it
Cares for

I sit with my moms
Mama watches a documentary about the sea
Mum reads a magazine about knitting

I just sit
And watch them
And try to imagine them
Without the shop
What would they do?
I can't picture them
At other jobs
Sitting in offices
Or standing behind a counter
That isn't ours
That isn't filled with magic
I can't imagine our family
Without magic
Without the books
The beanbags they let Charlotte and me pick
The shelves they built
The regulars who come in and spend hours
Browsing and reading
Perusing
Searching
Reading spines and blurbs and oohing and aahing
Leaving with books clutched to their chests
Ready for new adventures
I would miss them
Sandy
Who reads sci fi
And knows just about everything about space
Frankie who reads history and collects books
    about famous ships

Ash who comes in for travel guides before all of
    her trips
And tells us all about all the countries she's been
    to
Willow who's just a couple years older than me
Who reads mystery books and tries to piece all
    the clues together before the characters do
What if we never saw them again?
I would miss them
I would miss everything

'Why is Charlotte so mad?'
I ask eventually
Deciding that silence
Isn't helping
Mum sighs
And Mama says she isn't really sure
That maybe
Charlotte is just protective of the shop
I just shrug
That can't be it
We're all protective of the shop
We wouldn't be mean to each other because of it
Would we?
It must be something else
And I must figure out what

Mama and I keep watching the movie
And she keeps
Getting distracted

As dolphins and pufferfish swim across the screen
So I hold her hand
And squeeze it a little
And she turns to me
And smiles
But it doesn't reach the whole way up
To her eyes
So I squeeze her hand a little more
A little harder
As if to say
It's OK
It's all OK
But really
I don't know if it is
I don't tell her about the book in Mum's bag
Though something tells me
She already knows
About that

The next morning
The shop is in disarray
Books are strewn across the floor
Shelves sit empty
The till keeps opening and closing by itself
Spewing coins onto the floor
The book still sits on the counter
Purple and yellow cover bright against the dark wood
I decide to pick it up but Mama scoops it up and
    puts it on the shelf behind her
Before I make a move

So I wander back to the kids' section
And start putting books back on their shelves

Today's stack is small
Six books
And we have to open late because of the mess
So Mum is more stressed than usual
People wander in and out
Someone buys a book about bees
Someone almost buys one about gardening
But changes their mind
Someone wants a classic about a very rich man
Who's in love with a very rich woman
But after the mess of the morning
We can't find it
Anywhere
And by the end of the day
We're all downtrodden and frustrated

We get pizza for dinner
Because no-one wants to cook or do dishes
We sit on the couch and the floor
And put a movie on
But no-one really watches it

After a while of quiet munching
I ask
'Do you think they'll ever show up?
The owner of the book?'

And Mum just shrugs
And Mama says she sure hopes so
And Charlotte says nothing at all
I try again
'Do you think it'll keep getting worse?
If they don't come get it?'
Mum shrugs
Mama says she sure hopes not
And Charlotte says nothing at all
And since it seems no-one else will
I decided to do something about it
To do something about all of it
The book
   the magic
       the money

I stay up late again
With my notebook and a pen again
My nightlight off and a torch in my hand
So no-one knows I'm still awake
I make a list
An important list
A list to fix everything
First things first
I need to get the book
I need to read it and know it and understand it
So I can find its person
Maybe it's just someone we've missed
Maybe it's even someone we know

And we've just not thought of them
When I've read the book I'll know exactly who to
    look for
I'm sure of it
Second of all
I need to secretly spread the word about our magic
I know the moms and Charlotte don't agree
But I just know
I just know
That sharing our magic will help us
So I'll find secret little ways to do it
And then
The more people know about the magic
The more people will turn up
The more books will be bought
The more the stack will grow and grow
Every single day
Then the moms won't have to worry
And I won't have to worry
And once everything is better
They'll know I was right to share our secret
I'm sure of it

The next morning
We're afraid to open the door to the shop
We've even come down early
Just in case we need to tidy again
But when we open the door
The shop is
Normal

Quiet
Just as we left it
No empty shelves
No books on the floor
No coins
It's just
Normal
Mum looks shocked
Mama looks relieved
Charlotte looks
Charlotte looks
I can't quite figure out how Charlotte looks
But she just pushes past me
And turns on the lights
And grabs a duster
And disappears in among the shelves
'Well'
Mum says
'Straight to work then I suppose!'
And we all let out a big sigh of relief
And smile at each other
And get to work

At lunch time
Before I head upstairs for a snack
I decide it's time
To sneak the book away
I wait until Mum is busy with a customer
And Mama is putting new books on the shelves
And I creep behind the counter and reach up

On my tippy toes
To grab the book from the shelf
But
But
When I reach up
There's nothing there

The book is gone

I tell Mum
'Mum'
I say
'The book
The mystery book
The lonely book
It's gone
Do you have it?'
And she shakes her head
And says
'Isn't it on the shelf?'
And I shake my head
And find Mama
'Mama'
I say
'Do you have the mystery book?'
And she shakes her head
And says
'Isn't it on the shelf?'
And I tell her no

It's gone
'Maybe ask Charlotte'
She suggests
And I'm nervous to try to talk to her
But I find her
Sitting on the couch
Writing in her journal
And I ask
'Hey
Have you seen the lonely book?'
And she doesn't even look up
Just mutters a low
'No'
And keeps writing
And I don't even think she's still mad at me
I don't think this is about me at all
I think there's something up with Charlotte
And I add it to the list in my head
The list of things I need to fix

The list is getting long
And that worries me
I worry about my family
My sister
The shop
Money
The mystery book
The lonely book
Although

Maybe the mystery book
Isn't a problem any more
I think
Maybe it's just gone
Maybe it just
Gave up
The thought makes me sad
But maybe
It's one less thing to worry about
I decide not to stress about the book today
To hope it's all OK
And I decide instead
To begin my plan
My plan to share our magic

I start with a regular:
Willow
She comes in after school
And goes straight to the mystery section
I go up to her and say hi
She smiles at me and says
'Got anything new?'
'Of course!'
I show her some of our newest mysteries
And she's so excited
It makes me feel all warm inside

After a little while
Mum comes up

A paperback in her hands
I recognise it from the stack
'What about this one?'
She says to Willow
And Willow gasps and squeals
'That's perfect!'
And Mum gives her a beaming smile
And wanders back over to the counter
I take a deep breath
'It's magic
You know'
I whisper
'What?'
Willow whispers back
'What's magic?'
'The books!'
I tell her
'The shop!'
She looks at me funny
'Yeah'
She says
'Bookshops are magic!'
And I nod
But I know she isn't getting it
'No!' I whisper
'I mean
Yes! Of course!
But this is *real* magic!'
She looks at me

For a few long seconds
Then
'Cool'
She says
And walks towards the counter
She gives me a kind smile
And a wave
And says thanks for helping
But I know
She didn't believe me

Next I try with a woman pushing a buggy
'This shop is magic
You know'
I whisper
Conspiratorially
Like I'm a spy
But then her baby starts crying and she ignores me

I try to tell a little kid
But he just says
'And I'm a unicorn!'
And starts prancing around me

I try and I try
But no-one listens
No-one believes me

Not the man with the dog
Or the kid with the long hair

Not the woman with the tattoos
Or the person with the dungarees

No-one
No-one
No-one

I can't believe I thought that would work
I can't believe I thought anyone would
Listen to
Me

And can I blame them
I know it sounds
Silly
Magic
I know I sound
Silly
But I'm not
I'm just lucky
And I just want to share
That luck
What is so wrong
With that?

At lunchtime
Mama notices that I'm down
Sullen
'What's wrong, bug?'
She asks

Handing me a sandwich
And sneaking some extra crisps
Onto the side of my plate

'Just
Thinking about the book'
I lie
Kind of lie
Lie a little

She sighs
'It's such a sad little thing
Isn't it'
She sits next to me
Steals one of my crisps
And says
'Maybe it's on an adventure'
And gives me a smile
That makes me want to believe
Just that

I decide to try notes next
'Hello!
We have magic!
Come again!'
I write it on our Birch Books bookmarks
And slip them into random books
Throughout the shop
I put them in some popular thrillers

Some chunky fantasy books
Some poetry
Some picturebooks
I sneak around the shop
Trying not to look
Suspicious
Hiding them between pages
Whispering to them to please
Please work

I watch the books all day
Tiptoeing back and forth
Between sections
Watching and waiting
For someone to pick them up
For someone to flip through a book
And find a bookmark
And gasp in delighted surprise
And dash out to share the news with
Everyone they know
But I guess I chose the wrong books

I drop into a beanbag
Defeated
Dejected
Hoping against hope
That someone will take one of the books home
Will find the note
And will come back

Excited about our magic
Excited about our books
Excited to share it all
They'll come back with all their friends
And the stack will be so high it reaches the ceiling

The day has been slow and peaceful
When Mama took us
Upstairs for lunch
Charlotte disappeared
Into her room
But that's OK
Mama and I eat our sandwiches
Together and
Come up with more and more
Implausible ideas about
What happened to the
Lonely book
Maybe it sprouted legs
And ran away
Maybe a ninja stole it
Maybe aliens abducted it
We giggle over our toasties
And I think about
How much I love her
How lucky I feel
To have people who can cheer me up
To have two moms
Who love me and
Soothe me and laugh with me
And a sister
A Charlotte
Who might vanish into her
Room sometimes

But who is everything
Everything
Anyone could want in
A sister
A sibling
A best friend

The rest of the day
At the shop
Is tough
My head hurts a little
And my words don't want to come
I try to suggest books for customers
Here!
Try this book about a lizard!
Here!
Try this book about a whale!
Here! Here! Here!
But it's harder than usual
The books and I aren't
Connecting
I think

Mama says I should go upstairs
And lie down
But I don't want to be alone
I feel off
Delicate
Breakable
I want to be with my family

I want to be
Together

I go quiet all evening
I try to talk
I do
But it just
Doesn't work
Sometimes
It makes me feel
Claustrophobic
Like I'm stuck in myself
So I sit
And read
And journal
Surround myself with words
To remind myself that
Mine will come back

Charlotte softens
She smiles at me more
She even looks a little
Apologetic
She asks me about the book I'm reading
And I try to sign back to her
But I'm still learning sign language
So I sign slowly
But she doesn't seem to mind
She sits on the floor at my feet
Her dress fanning out around her

And she watches my hands intently
And something inside me
Loosens
Warms
And for a few minutes
I have one less thing to worry about

Charlotte
Is kind
Charlotte is
Good
A Good Person
The Best Person
Charlotte hugs me every morning
Charlotte helps me with my signing
Charlotte helps me breathe when it's hard
Charlotte reads to me
Books she thinks I'll like
Funny scenes
Insightful quotes
Charlotte gives me the biggest slice of pizza
Charlotte lets me sleep in her bed when I have
Nightmares
Rubs my tummy when I'm sick
Laughs at my favourite shows with me
Holds my hand when I'm scared
Charlotte
Is kind
Charlotte is
Good

A Good Person
The Best Person

I stay up late again
After Mum and Mama kiss me goodnight
And Charlotte hugs me and ruffles my curls
I try to sleep
Really I do
But I just
Can't
I have too much in my head
Too many stuck words
Too many worries

So my plan didn't work
So what
That was only the first try
I only need one person to believe me
Then they can tell someone
And they can tell someone
And they and they and they
And then our shop will be so busy
We'll run out of books
OK maybe not that busy
But busy enough that
Mum won't have to stress any more
Yes
I'll try again tomorrow
I'll try and I'll try and I'll
Try

Mum and I are up early the next morning
On Saturdays we always make a special breakfast
Pancakes and strawberries and syrup
Hot chocolate with marshmallows
Mum and I like to cook together
So we get up first and get flour all over our pyjamas
Sugar in our hair
We like cooking together
But we are not very good at it

While I'm slicing strawberries
I decide to ask about the book
'Mum'
I say
'Yes'
She says
'You know the book?'
I say
'Yes'
She says
'What is it about?'
'Well,'
She says
'It's about gender'
Gender
I think
'Why would you need a whole book about gender?
Isn't it just boy and girl?
How much more is there to say?'
I ask her

And she takes a breath and says
'Well
Not exactly
You see'
She says
'When we are born
The doctors tell our parents
Congratulations!
It's a boy!
Or
Congratulations!
It's a girl!
But sometimes
They're wrong'

'Wrong?
How could that be?'
She stops mixing the pancake batter
And looks at me
Her face kind and her eyes bright and I love my
    Mum
Because she looks me in my eyes
And she explains
Not like I'm a little kid
But like I'm a someone
A someone who could learn and understand

'Sometimes
People who are told they're boys
Are actually girls

And sometimes
People who are told they're girls
Are actually boys
They're *transgender*
That's the word
*Transgender*'
She repeats
And I say it too
Let the idea take root in my head

'How do they know?'
I ask
And Mum says
'I suppose they just do
The way you know yourself
You know lots of things about yourself
So do they
And it's one of the things they know'
She smiles
And I smile back
'Do we know any transgender people?'
I ask
And she nods
'You know Mama's friend Amy?'
I nod
'She's trans'
Oh
I didn't know
I've always known Amy

My whole life
And I've always known her as a girl
A woman
That makes sense
Of course she's a woman!
It's pretty cool
I think
That people can be
Exactly who they are
Even if the doctors are wrong at the beginning
Even if everyone is wrong

'So that's what the book is about?'
'Not just that'
She tells me
'There's more
Sometimes
People don't feel like a girl
Or a boy
Sometimes
They feel like they exist
Somewhere in the middle
Here's a new word, Annie
They're *non-binary*
That's how they *identify*'
'What does identify mean?' I ask
'It means
Well
It means how they see themselves

How they think of themselves
How they feel they are in the world
Not one
Or the other
Something else
So they *identify* as that something
And that something else is called ...'
'Non-binary'
That sounds cool
I think
*Non-binary*
'Sometimes
Non-binary people use different pronouns'
'Pronouns?'
'So *you* is a pronoun
*I* is a pronoun
*She* is a pronoun
*He* is a pronoun
You did pronouns at school?'
I nod
We did
'So, instead of being called *he* or *she*
Non-binary people often like to be called *they*
      and *them*
Or even other pronouns sometimes'
She explains
'People are amazing'
She says
'We can be so many things

Express ourselves in so many ways
There's more to gender
People who are both
People who are neither
People who feel one way one day
And differently the next
It's a *spectrum*!
A whole rainbow!
We are all
Exactly who we are
And it's all
Completely and
Totally
OK'

It's a lot to take in
A whole world of possibilities
Of identities
Of selves
But ...
It's
Exciting
Isn't it?
To know
You
And I
Can be
Whoever
We are

Exactly
Who
We are

It *is* exciting

I feel this new knowledge
Settle in me
And it's warm
It's a comfy weight
Like a full tummy
After a lovely meal
It sits in me
And I'm so happy to have it

'So'
I ask after a minute
'If I was a boy
Or non-binary
Or another ... *identity*?'
'Yes, that's the word'
'Would that be OK
With you and Mama?'
Mum takes my face in her hands
And says
'Of course
Of course
Of course'

'Charlotte!'
I squeal
And she turns and smiles at me
All cosy in her pyjamas
Book in her hands
'A Tale of Love and Lore'
It has a woman on the front
Holding a rose and looking forlorn
I jump into Charlotte's arms
I'm buzzing with my new information
My new way of seeing things
Charlotte laughs
'Why are you so hyper?' she asks
And hugs me
Pulling me onto the couch beside her
'Mum just taught me the coolest stuff'
I tell her
And she says
'Oh?'
Slipping a bookmark into her book and
Giving me her full
Fullest attention
'Yeah'
I start
'Did you know
You don't have to be only a girl or a boy?'
She pales a little
'What do you mean?'
She asks

Gripping her book
In her hands
'Some people are non-binary!'
I tell her
'It means they exist outside the idea of just boy or
   girl
They don't *identify* as just boy or girl
Isn't that interesting?'
I tell her all about what Mum told me
How gender can be a spectrum
Not just two options
How people can identify however they feel
I talk and talk
I love learning new things
I love learning that things are bigger than I
   thought they were
That the world is big big big
And full of people
Living in so many different ways
Being who they are
Loving who they love
Doing what they want
I love learning
All the things I could be and do and feel and see
All the options
I love it
I love feeling
Like a tiny part
Of a big big world

Charlotte says that that's cool
She puts a hand on my cheek
And looks into my eyes
And says
'Love you Annie'
And she gets up
And she goes to her room
And I sit
And I wonder what happened
She didn't look
Sad
Exactly
Or happy
Exactly
She looked
Like she was full of feelings
Like she couldn't choose one to feel fully

Mum and I finish making the pancakes
And I try not to worry about Charlotte
She's been acting
Different
Recently
She's quiet
Not quiet like me
Not quiet like she has things to say
But quiet like she has secrets to keep

It's starting to feel
Like everyone has
A secret
And it's starting to feel
A little
Lonely
Charlotte is quiet
All the time
And the moms are stressed
All the time
And the shop is acting
All anxious and wrong and
I'm just
Here

I try to push it all away
I try to tell myself I'm being
Silly
Dramatic
   Dramatic
       Dramatic

I sit at the table
With a pile of pancakes up to my chin
And a smile on my face
Maybe it's a little forced
But I smile my smile anyway

We make too many pancakes
And we eat too many pancakes

And we laugh and chat and look forward to the day
And I cross my fingers under the table
Ask the day
Please
Let the shop be peaceful
The magic
Settled
The day
Hopeful

When we get to the shop
The sun is shining
And we are light

Mum unlocks the door and we march inside
Happy and ready and
The shop is in disarray
Books everywhere
Shelves knocked over
The book
The mystery book
The lonely book
Is sitting on the counter

'No'
I gasp
And dart towards the counter
'How is it back?'
Mum lets out a big sigh
Stepping over books

Tiptoeing her way to me
She takes the book from the counter
Turns it over
Looks at the spine
'Hmm'
She murmurs
'The spine is broken
Looks like someone read it'

All day the shop is chaos
We put books back on the shelves
And they fly off again

The shop is mad
I think
Angry that it got what it needed
And now it's taken
A giant step
Back

I wish I could help it
I wish I could make it
Feel better

I wish I could make everyone feel better
Mum is stressed
Mama is full of worry
Charlotte is
I don't know what Charlotte is feeling
She's worried about the shop

Of course
She's flustered all day
Catching books before they fall
And putting them back
Over and over

All day I wonder who took the book
But I don't have much time to really think about it
Running around all day trying to keep
The chaos controlled
And hidden from customers
After a while Charlotte and I are
Exhausted
And Mum and Mama tell us to go read
Not to worry about the shop
Which is easier said than done

Charlotte is quiet
For the rest of the day
She mostly sits
And reads
In the comfy chair
Beside the classics
Absentmindedly
Pushing back books that slide out around her
Every now and then

For a while
I sit at her feet
And read about a mouse

Going on a big adventure
The shop is quiet today
So our moms reorganise shelves
While we read
And every time the door
Tinkles
We all look up
Wondering if this next person
Will be
The person
If this next person
Will take the book
In their hands
And smile
And nod
And the mystery will be solved
And everything will go back to
Normal

I try to look
For the owner of
The book

I look at everyone who comes into the shop
I look at their faces
Their clothes
The way they move
The way they walk
But I realise
Pretty quickly

That I don't know what a non-binary person
Looks like
Or dresses like
Or moves or walks like
And maybe
I think
They don't look or dress or move
Any particular way

How am I to find them?
How am I to find the owner?

I try talking to people
I say
'Hello!
How are you!'
And eventually
'Are you interested in a book about
Non-binary identities?'

Some give me funny looks
Some say no
Some say yes but don't buy the book
Some say no I don't agree with that
Which I don't understand
And some say no thank you
I already understand!

Everyone has a different answer
But none is the right one

No-one says
'Yes please!
I've been looking for this!
Waiting for this!
Hoping for this!'

I only need one
Only one
But that one
Doesn't come

I see Mama
Flipping through the book
At the counter
While the shop is quiet
She even writes
Some things down
And I wonder what she's learning
And I hope she
Shares it all

I am confident
I am
Sometimes
When people see me go
Quiet
Or see me get a little
Panicked
They think I must be
Quiet
All the time
That I must be scared
All the time
But I'm not
I know myself
And what I'm capable of
Sometimes
Things are just
A little harder
Is all

But I do my breathing exercises
And I practise my sign language
And I talk to my family when I'm down or scared
    or anxious
And I see a therapist
Miss Kate
Every week
And I know
        I know

I'll be
OK

Miss Kate
Says she is
Proud of me
That I'm dealing well
With the change of pace
Change of routine
That summer brought
Sometimes
That's hard for me

I wish I could tell her about the book and the shop
    and the magic
But I know I can't
I know she wouldn't believe me
I know it would make her worry
I know my family wouldn't be happy
So I don't say
Anything

It's hard
Trying to be honest about everything
While having to keep secrets
But I try
I talk about seeing Mum take the big book
With the euros on the cover
I talk about what I think that means
I talk about how much that scares me

How much I love the way our life is right now
How I don't want it to change

I feel
A little
Lighter
Afterwards
Looser
Relieved
A little less
Weighed down

Still
I feel
A little
Like I've betrayed Mum
Telling her secret to someone
But Miss Kate says
This is my space
My time
That I can say
Whatever I need to say
That it's safe and OK

Miss Kate says it's important
Not to carry things around
Not to fill myself up with worries
That I need
To get it all out
She reminds me

That I'm a kid
I'm the kid
I shouldn't be anxious about
Adult things
Adult matters
Adult stresses
It isn't my responsibility
It isn't for me to fix
But I can't help it
I'm still a little
Worried
About Mum
About the shop
About the future

Miss Kate says I should trust
Mum
Trust that she's an adult
She's the adult
That she knows what she's doing
That she can fix this
Without me
But Miss Kate
Didn't see her face
Didn't hear her sighs
I know she's right
I know Mum
Is the grown-up
But what if she can't
What if she can't?

Mama takes me for hot chocolate
After my therapy session
We sit in our favourite coffee shop
And we dunk our marshmallows
Under the whipped cream
And we laugh at our milk moustaches


'How was your session?'
Mama asks when we've stopped giggling
I sigh
'It was OK'
I tell her
'Miss Kate says I worry too much'
'What are you worried about?'
But I can't tell her
I can't tell her about Mum
The big book
The shop
I can't tell her I'm scared we'll lose
Everything
And I couldn't tell Miss Kate about the mystery
    book
So I can't say that either
'Charlotte'
I say
Because it might not be my truest truth
But it's pretty far from a lie


'Me too'
Mama smiles sadly

'But I know Charlotte
I know how strong
How resilient
How capable
She is
I know
I *know*
That whatever Charlotte is going through
Whatever Charlotte is working through
Right now
She can get through it
I know
I *know*
Charlotte
I know
I *know*
Charlotte will be OK'

And for the first time
Hearing Mama's words
Hearing how sure they are
Seeing her smile
Feeling her holding my hand
I feel like
Everything else
Will be OK
Too

There's a woman in the business section
The woman looks sad
A deep-down heavy kind of sad
She sits on the couch
A pile of books beside her
And she leafs through them
A certain type of desperation
Surrounding her like smoke
I watch her
Over the top of my book
Settled in my beanbag and
Worried worried worried
She doesn't seem to see me watching her
She just picks up book after book
And places them back down moments later
With a little sigh
Or a furrow of her brow
After a while I stop spying
Wrestle my way out of my beanbag
And wander over
Feeling brave
Feeling my words
Sitting ready on my tongue

'Hello'
I say
She jumps a little
'Oh'

She says
'Hello'
'Can I help you?'
I ask
And she smiles a little
And shakes her head
'Are you sure?'
I say
'I know a lot about books!'
She smiles a little bigger and says
'That's great
But I'm beginning to think the answers I need
Don't live in books'
I want to say that's silly
But I don't
I just say
'Books have all the answers!
You just have to find the right book!'
'Well'
She says
And looks down
'I need a book about
Losing things
About having to say goodbye
Before you're ready
About loneliness'
'Oh'
I say
'Hmm'
I hum

Well
I scratch my head
Thinking hard
Then
'I'll be right back'
She smiles
But it's a sad smile

I go to the stack
One of them has to belong to this woman
I just know it
There's a gardening book
And a cookbook
And a children's classic
I'm halfway through the stack
When Mum appears
And I sigh in relief
'Mum!
We need to help this woman!'
Mum laughs
'OK OK'
She says
'Calm down
What woman?
Help with what?'
I tell her about the lady
About how sad she is
About how she needs answers
About how she's lost something
And needs our help

Mum nods along
Then says
'OK
OK'
And looks through the stack
She slides out a big hardback book
And takes my hand

We make our way over to the couch
And the woman is still there
Flipping through a small purple book
She sighs and puts it down then looks up
And gives us a shy smile
'Hello'
My Mum says
And gives her her kindest smile
Which is very
Very kind
And could make just about
Anyone
Feel better
I'm sure of it

They sit together
And I sit on the floor
And they talk
And they talk
And they talk about
Losing things

About the pain of it
The sadness
The loneliness
The woman says she had a shop
A shop her mother had opened
And a shop
She had to close
Had to say goodbye to
Had to walk away from
And I see
My Mum's face
Change
Just a little
Get a little sadder

'That must have been very difficult'
Mum says
Gently
'Yes
It was'
Says the woman
'It's hard
Isn't it'
Mum says
Looking down
'Keeping going
Keeping things
Moving'

The woman takes both of her hands
And they look at each other
And I look away
Because it feels
Private

After a minute
My Mum takes a deep breath
And says
'You will be OK
You have done nothing wrong
You have not failed
You will be
OK'

And the woman nods
And says
'We will be OK'
And Mum nods

And silently
And full of hope
Just to myself
I nod too

At home that night
I help make the shepherd's pie
And I try to decide how to bring up
The woman
And Mum

And the way they
Shared the same
Fear and worry
And the way I saw that fear and worry
And the way I felt it
And the way
I want to help
The way I want to make sure
Mum never feels that
Again

Mum washes the potatoes
Mama stirs the mince
I chop the carrots
Charlotte sets the table
We are a well-oiled machine
A perfect team
We are

But I can't figure out how to
Bring up
What happened
I wonder if Mum has told Mama
I wonder if Mama knows about the book in Mum's
    bag
I wonder I wonder I wonder
Does Charlotte know we're in trouble
Or is it only me
And Mum?
A secret we carry

Together
But alone

After dinner we go to sign-language class
We learn new words
New phrases
New ways of communicating
And as always
I feel powerful
I feel safe
I feel loved

I brought the lonely book
Home with me
Hidden under my jumper
I know
Maybe
I shouldn't have
But I did
But I had to

I slip it under my pillow
To read by my night light
Tonight
When everyone is asleep
Maybe
I think
If I get to know
The book

If I understand it
Maybe
That'll help me find
The person who needs it

I sneak the book out from
Under my pillow
The cover is purple and yellow and happy looking
The inside is intimidating
Small print and long words and no pictures
Still
I try
I read the back first
It promises to explain
Identities
Non-binary
Genderqueer
Gender non-conforming
Words I wouldn't have recognised before
But want to learn
All about
Now

Maybe
I think
If I can understand the book
And all it has to say
It'll be easier to find its person
I open the book to page one

And decide to try
My best

The next day in the shop
I sneak the book back onto the counter
Before anyone notices it ever left
I read as much as I could before I fell asleep
I learned about all sorts of people
I didn't know about before
People who were told they were boys
When really they were girls
On the inside
Where it counts
People who were told they were girls
When really they were boys
People who are both
People who are neither
People who are somewhere in between
It was fascinating
It made the world feel
Bigger

The bookshop is even worse
Every day it's changing
Every day it's getting
Worse and
Worse and
Worse
And it's spreading
It's seeping into our heads
The wrongness
The unease
Everyone is getting crankier
Everyone is getting
Impatient
Even unkind
Sometimes
We're all stressed and scared
For our shared reason
And for all our own

The magic
Usually so quiet and secretive
Thrums and hums and crackles
And we all feel it
The lonely book lies on the counter
Watching books come and go while it just
Sits
Unclaimed
Unwanted

It starts to feel like a ghost
Haunting the shop
Its presence
Thick and heavy

The day's new stack is nine books
And they keep jumping from the counter
Or flipping open
Pages fluttering like the feathers of an angry
    swan
They too
Know something is wrong

As the days go by
The magic grows more
Unsettled
Books fly from shelves
The bell above the door
Rings and rings

The moms are worried
I can tell
But they try their best to act
Like everything is fine

I hear them fight
No
not fight
Not exactly

I hear them
Whispering
Loud whispers
Angry whispers

They're in the kitchen
And I'm in the sitting room
And I shouldn't be listening
I shouldn't
I know
I *know*
But I can't help it
I can't hear much anyway
Not everything
Just
Bits
And pieces

'You should've told me anyway'
And
'How bad'
And
'I'm sorry'

I go to bed early
Hide under the covers
With my favourite book
With its pretty cover
And its illustrations

And its story I know
So well
About brave little animals
And a kind little girl
And a big adventure

I try to read
I try to be
Comforted
I try to go away
To a different world
To a world without
Forgotten books and fighting moms and sad sisters
But it doesn't work
It doesn't
Work

After a few hours
When I've given up
I sneak into Charlotte's room
Tiptoe my way across her plush carpet
And crawl under the covers
'Hey, bug'
She whispers
Her voice sleepy and heavy and quiet
'What's wrong?'
Of course she knows something's wrong
Of course of course
Because she is my big sister

And she knows me better than just about
Anyone
I shuffle close to her
As she wraps her arms around me
'Nightmares?'
She asks
And I mumble a no
'Is it the shop?'
'Kind of'
I whisper
'It's just'
I wonder if I should tell her about the book
Mum's book
With the euro signs all over it
But I don't want to worry her
So I decide not to
No no no
She's been quiet enough lately
Whatever is going on for Charlotte
I won't make it worse
I will hold this worry
Close to me
Tight in my fists
Hot in my chest
I will carry it
I hug her
And I whisper
'It's nothing
Can I sleep here?'

And she sighs sleepily
And says of course
And two minutes later
She's fast asleep again

The shop is still unhappy
It seems
Bitter
Maybe
That it got what it wanted
Then had it taken away
Maybe
We all feel a little
Bitter
That things were better
Maybe we didn't have answers
But we had peace
For a little while
And ever since then
It's just
Deteriorated and
Deteriorated
And now
Now the shop
Is angrier than ever

'We might have to close for the day'
Mum yells over the crashing of the till drawer
Zooming in and out
'But we can't'
Mama yells back
Trying and failing to keep books
From flying from shelves

'But someone could get hurt'
Charlotte yells
Trying to catch a beanbag
Rolling across the floor
Like a giant dust bunny

I stand in the middle of the shop
Watching the chaos
Trying to breathe
Trying to speak
Trying to
Help
But I can't
All I can do
Is stand
Here
There
Stand
And watch
And wish
Things would
Just get
Better

I feel like the shop
I feel wrong deep inside
I feel like I want to throw things too
Want to make a mess
Want to yell

Why can't things just stay
The way they are?
Why can't things just stay
The way they are
Meant to be?

'Stop'
I sign
But no-one sees

We closed the shop early and
We're playing a board game
One with elves and dwarves and magicians
I'm not sure who's winning
But I know we're having fun

Suddenly I can't breathe
The evening has been normal
Usual
Fine
We made dinner together
We read on the couch
We watched a funny show
Normal
Usual
Fine
　Normal
　　　　Usual
　　　　　　Fine

Suddenly I can't breathe
I'm thinking about my family
I'm thinking about Charlotte
Who doesn't seem mad at me any more
But who doesn't seem
At peace
Who seems
Like she's carrying something

Something invisible and heavy
And not meant
To be carried
Alone

Suddenly I can't breathe
I'm looking at my moms
At Mum with her big secret book
Her big secret
And Mama
With her worried eyes
And fidgety hands

Suddenly I can't breathe
I can feel the shop beneath my feet
Thrumming and vibrating
Full of magic it doesn't know what to do with
Broken by one little book
One little lonely book
Sitting on a counter
All alone
And the shop
In panicked chaos around it
Afraid it might be
Abandoned
And I feel it
In my bones
Its power
Its love for us

It's part of us
As we are
Of it
We can't
Leave it
Behind

Suddenly
I can't
Breathe

I grab Mum's hand
Squeeze it tight
So tight
And she looks at me
And she squeezes back
And she puts her hand on my cheek
And she says
In
Hold
Out
  In
  Hold
  Out
     In
     Hold
     Out

And I breathe

In

Hold

Out

And I breathe
And I breathe
And I breathe

And when I'm breathing
Like normal
Again
Mum says
'What's wrong?'
With her eyes and her words
And her hand in mine
Squeezing squeezing squeezing
Never too tight
Always just
Right

And Mama slides over to us
And puts her arms around me
And I snuggle into her
And feel her warmth
Her softness
I hear her heart in her chest
And I let it
Calm me
I let my moms
Calm me
Care for me
Love me
And I feel safe
And I'm breathing

Breathing
Breathing
In and out and OK OK OK
And I figure
It's probably time
I let myself
Let go
A little
Of everything
I'm carrying
Around

I can't bring myself to say it
I want them to know I know
I want them to know I'm scared
I want them to know I'm desperate to help
Desperate for things to stay
Just the way they are
The way they were
I open my mouth
But nothing comes out
I don't know what to say
Or how to say it
And I don't know that I could
Even if I did know
   What to say
       Or how to say it
If I could
   If I could
I would say please

Please let me help
Please tell me how
But I know
Even if I could say it
They would say
It isn't for me to fix
That it isn't my
Responsibility
But I know
I know I know
If we lose it all
The shop the home the magic
And I did nothing to stop it
It'll feel
All my
Fault

I use my hands
I use what I've learned
'I'm
Scared'
I sign
'I feel
Worried'
Mum and Mama look surprised
And a little confused
And a lot concerned
Why?
Mama signs back

Making a C shape with her pointer and thumb
and placing it on her chest
I take a deep breath
A big breath
The deepest breath
And I sign
'I know
I know we are in
Trouble'

Mum moves from the couch and kneels in front of
    me
'What do you mean
Trouble?'
She whispers
And her eyes look so big
So round
So close to tears
I hug her tight
Arms around her neck
Tummy pressed into her
I hug her and hug her and hug her and I don't
Let go
'I know the shop is in trouble'
I whisper
'I know we need more money
We need more customers
We need more and more
I know'

She squeezes me tight
'Annie'
Mama says from the couch
'This isn't for you to worry about
Sweetheart'
I nod
'I know'
I say
'But
I am
So really
Does it
Matter'
Mama nods
And sighs
'I guess not'
She says
'I'm sorry you're so worried'
She says
'I promise
I promise
Mum and I are doing everything we can to save
    the shop
I promise'

But I know
That isn't true
Not really
Not as true
As it could be

I don't say so
But I feel
A bitterness inside
A sourness
Tangy and acrid and horrible
I want to yell
I realise
And it shocks me
I want to yell
I want to yell at them
At my parents
My moms
At Charlotte
At everyone
We have
This gift
We are
So
So lucky
And if we were just
If we were only
Brave enough
To share it
To show it
Then everything
Everything!
Would be
Better
Different
Better

Better.

Charlotte comes out of her room
While Mum is still hugging me
And Mama is watching us
Concern and love
Fighting on her face
'What's wrong?'
Charlotte asks
And Mama says
'Come here, baby'
And Charlotte wanders over
Straight into Mama's arms
'The shop'
Mama starts
'Isn't doing so well
At the minute
And Annie
Is a little scared
About what's going to happen'

'What is going to happen?'
Charlotte asks
Eyes wide
And darting from Mum to Mama to me
'Nothing
Nothing
We'll sort it out
We will

Sort it out'
Mama says each word
Like they matter
Like saying them loud and sure will fill them with
    power
Will make them true and strong and unbreakable
We will
Sort it
Out

'Now I just wish
We could figure out the
Book'
I say
We can't really share our magic
If it's going haywire
Can we?
'Me too'
Mum says
'But what can we do about it
Really?'
Mama asks
'We can't just get rid of the book
We can't just sell it to someone it doesn't belong to
What can we do?'
Suddenly
Charlotte stands up
And takes a deep breath
And looks at each of us

She starts to say something
Then shakes her head a little and
Mutters
'I love you guys
I love you so much
And really
I think we're going to be
OK'
And Mama takes her hand
And they share a look
And Mum looks at me
And we share a look
Then we all hug again
And it's time for bed

I'm exhausted
Panicking
Always makes me
So tired
Bone-tired
Heavy
Heavy-tired
But I feel
A little better
At the same time
Mum tucks me into bed
And as I look up at her
I realise
I feel a little
Calmer

I feel like
A little weight
Has fallen
From my shoulders

Mum tells me she loves me
She tells me she's proud of me
She tells me things she tells me
All the time
But they feel
Even more
True
Tonight

The next morning I decide
To try again
One more time
I decide
One more time

I let everyone finish their toast
Then I stand up
I can do this
I think
I can speak
Loud and sure
I can do
This

Everyone looks at me
And I feel myself
Get a little
Shy
But they are my family
And they love me
Every bit as much as I love them
Which is a lot
A lot a lot
They won't judge me
They won't be mean to me
They will listen

I tell myself
And I can speak
I tell myself
I can speak

'I know'
I start
'I know
You guys said
No'
I'm shaking a little
But I'm sure
I'm strong
I'm confident
'But I really think
We need to share
The magic
We have this beautiful thing
This thing that makes us
Special
I don't understand why we have to hide
That
Why hide what makes you different?
What makes you
You
The magic is a gift
From the shop to us
Mum said!
The shop felt so much love

It loved back
The best way it could
And maybe it's been
A little
Difficult
Recently
But it's trying its best!
There's no shame in being special.
Unique'

Charlotte is staring at me
Blinking a lot
Like she's thinking
Really hard

Mum and Mama are looking at each other
Doing that silent communicating thing
They do

I'm standing in front of them all
Nervous
But proud

'Isn't that what you've always told me?'
I look at my moms
Who always tell me to be proud of myself
Who tell me never to hide who I am
Never to feel shame
Or embarrassment

About what makes me me
What makes me special
Who are so
Proud of me
It makes me
Proud of me
Too

Mum smiles at me
And says
'Maybe
We should talk about this later
It's almost time to open the shop'
I nod
It isn't a no
So for now
I'll take it

Charlotte holds my hand as we leave the apart-
    ment
All the way down the stairs
To the shop
She squeezes a little
And I squeeze back
And I'm so glad
So relieved
So lucky
That she's my
Family

We unlock the door
Expecting
Some books on the floor
Some change scattered
Across the counter
We don't expect
Books
Flying
Around the
Room
Swooping from wall to wall
Dipping and diving
Shelves
Banging against the walls
Thud thud thud
The rotating stands are spinning so fast they
Could take off
The shop is chaos
Complete
Utter chaos

'What do we do?'
I yell
Over the banging of the shelves
And the whooshing of the books
'I don't know' Mama shouts back
Ducking to avoid a hardback
'How do we stop it?'
Mum shouts
Lunging to catch a Birch Books mug

Before it crashes to the ground
Charlotte stands in the doorway
Staring at the chaos
I'm jumping to catch books
Mama is trying to hold shelves still
Mum is catching things as they jump from stands
We're all
Panicked
And flustered
And a little scared
What if it never stops?
I think
What if it keeps getting worse?
What if the whole building falls!

I look at Charlotte
Who hasn't said anything yet
And I stop what I'm doing
Charlotte is smiling
She's watching the shop
The swirling and flying and smashing
And she's smiling
Charlotte looks
Peaceful
Charlotte looks
Sure

'Don't you see?'
She laughs
'It's different this time!

It's not mad or sad or scared
Don't you see?
This is joy
This is
Pride'

We all stop
And look
And she's right
The books are twirling
And swirling
Not crashing and bashing
The shelves are bouncing
Not thumping
Things aren't falling to the ground
They're leaping into the air
They aren't mad
They aren't sad
They are
Elated
They are
Excited
They are
Happy

Suddenly
Charlotte laughs a little
Then suddenly
She laughs a lot
She's bent over

Laughing and laughing
And we all stop
And we watch her
And we look at each other
And we're confused
And Mum looks a little worried
But Mama smiles at Charlotte
And then I do too

Charlotte stands up straight
Shoulders back
Chin up

She looks at each of us
With so much confidence
With so much love
With so much resolve

Charlotte takes a step into the shop
Then another
And another
She gets faster
Walking with
Power

She runs the last few steps to the counter
And she grabs the book
The mystery book
The lonely book with no owner
And she clutches it to her chest

And suddenly
The books stop flying
And slide themselves back onto the shelves
Which have stopped hitting the walls
The coins stop leaping from drawer to drawer
They zoom back into the till
And it shuts itself with a satisfying click
Everything rights itself
The bookmarks aren't spinning
On their rotating stands
The mugs aren't flying
The shop is at
Peace

'What just happened?'
I whisper into the silence
'I think I know'
Mama says
Beaming

Charlotte holds the book to her chest
She smiles down at it
Shyly
Like it's an old friend
She takes a deep breath
In hold out
In hold out
In hold out
Then she looks back up

Meets each of our eyes in turn
Smiles smiles smiles
And says

'It's mine
It's for me'
'It's yours'
I repeat
Charlotte nods
'I wasn't sure
But now I am!
The book helped'
She smiles
And looks at each of us

'I'm non-binary'
She says
Then smiles
Even bigger
'Oh'
I say
'Cool'
And I smile too
'Wow!'
Says Mum
And she smiles too
'OK'
Says Mama
And she smiles too

'I'd like you to start using
They/them pronouns for me'
They say
Full of confidence

'Of course'
Mama says
And we all nod
And nod and nod
'And
I'd like it if you could
Call me
Charlie'
Charlie says
'Of course'
Says Mum
And we're all nodding again
Charlie lets out a big
Breath
And they look so
Relieved
That I smile even bigger

A thought comes to me
But I think it's a bad one
So I bite my tongue
Charlie
Of course
Notices
'What's wrong?'

They ask
And I shake my head
'Come on'
They say
And poke me in the side
I giggle then mumble
'But
You like dresses
And
And
Pink
And'
Charlie laughs
'Being non-binary
Doesn't mean
You look a certain way
Or like certain things
I can wear dresses
And make-up and
Like cute pink things
And still be non-binary
Just as much as I could
If I liked blue or black
Or jeans or combat boots
Anyone
Who looks or acts
Any way
Can identify
However
They identify'

And that makes sense
And I know
I knew
That girls can be anything they want
And boys can be anything they want
So of course
Of course
It makes sense
That everyone else
Can too


'So you took the book?
That day the shop was calm?'
I ask
And they nod
'Yep
I took it and read it
Well
First I tried to get rid of it
I thought of maybe donating it to a charity shop
Giving it to someone else
Even throwing it out
    Which felt very, very wrong!
But ...
I knew it was meant for me
I knew it was time to learn and
Understand myself better
It was scary
I didn't know if I was ready

But once I took it home
And actually read it
I knew
I was ready
I was!
Maybe not to talk about it quite yet
Not until now
But ready to accept it
To accept myself
I saw myself in those pages
I saw everything I am and
Everything I could be
It made me feel
Excited
And full of
Hope'
They smile
And I haven't seen them look so
Light
In such a long time
I could cry
But only the
Happiest tears

'It helped a lot!'
They laugh a little
And Mama says
'Maybe we should read it too'
And Charlie looks at her

And says
'You would do that?'
And Mama looks surprised
And she says
'Of course!
Of course'
And Charlie nods
And wipes their eyes a little
And says
'That would be good
That would be
Nice'
And Mama scoops them up
And holds them tight
Mum and I pile on top of them both
And we all
Hold each other
Tight tight tight
Together together
Together

'I thought it would be
Scarier'
Charlie says
When we've all
Detangled ourselves
'I thought it would feel
Impossible
I thought sharing what made me

Me
Would make people
Love me less
Would be
A bad
Bad
Thing
But it isn't
But it wasn't
It feels good
And I know
I'm lucky
To have you guys
To be loved and accepted
No matter what
But maybe
We can spread this
Maybe
Like Annie says
We should share our magic
Maybe
We should share
What makes us
Us
Then
Maybe
When more people come
Maybe we can be here
To love

To accept
The people who
Aren't
Loved
And accepted
Elsewhere
Maybe we can use our magic
To make people
Feel safe
To give them somewhere
Where they can be
Themselves
No matter who
They are'

Mum smiles
Mama smiles
I smile
Charlie smiles
Mum nods
Mama nods
I nod
Charlie
Glows

I know who I am
That's what my moms say
Since day one
They insist
I've known who I am
I am Annie
I like books and my moms and my sibling
I am a girl
Though I don't like dresses or make-up like
Charlie does
I'm still a girl
I know that
I feel it
I am girl
Girl I am
I like the colour green
And potato waffles with beans
And I do not like celery
Or mean people
I am brave and strong and tall for my age
I take up my own little space in the world
And I do so proudly
I am Annie
And I like being Annie

Sometimes I try to imagine myself
As someone else
As someone

Who doesn't like
Being who
They are
It must feel
Lonely
I think
Not liking
Being with
Yourself
Feeling detached from who you are
Feeling separate from what people
See
From what the mirror
Sees

I wonder if that's what Charlie feels
Or felt
Or feels
I ask them
And they ruffle my hair
And say
That since we started using the right
Pronouns
Since we started using the right
Name
Everything has felt better
Which seems very
Bare minimum
To me
But they say it's been

Affirming
And that makes them happy
And that makes me happy
Too

Sometimes people still
Misgender
Them
In the shop
That means
They assume
Charlie is someone
They aren't
And they use the wrong words when speaking to
    them
But we just say
'Actually
This is Charlie!
They use they/them pronouns
Please use them when speaking about them'
And mostly people say
'Oh!
I'm sorry!'
And they learn
And they adjust
And they get it right the next time
And Charlie
Gets to just be
Charlie

# epilogue

The shop is full
The stack is tall
Charlie is laughing with a customer
Mum and Mama
Are holding hands behind the counter
Talking to two men
Holding hands on the other side of the counter
They're all smiling
Talking animatedly
I'm restocking the shelves
They empty so much faster now
We get boxes full almost every day
And we sell bunches every day
The shop has been doing
Wonderfully
Ever since we shared our magic
With customers
Old and new
Let them in
On our precious secret
And ever since we shared
Our love
Our kindness
Our tolerance

We've made new friends
We have lots of new regulars
We see people's shoulders drop when they walk in
   the door
We see them smile
We see them relax
People seem
At home
Here
Just like
Us

The shop is happy too
No books have fallen from shelves
No shelves have so much as shivered
Everything stays in place
Everything looks
Neat and shiny and lovely
The shop
Is happy

I'm happy too
Charlie is happy
And seeing them happy
Seeing them
So comfortable
So at peace
With themselves
With their life
With their world

Makes me feel
So proud
To know them
To love them
To be their little
Sister

My moms are happy too
They smile so much
They hold hands more
They haven't fought again
No secret whispers in the kitchen
No secrets at all

Sometimes I still go quiet
I might always go quiet
Sometimes
But we practice sign language
And we talk about things that worry me
And even when I'm
Quiet
I'm still
Me

No secrets between any of us
We are back to normal
We are better than normal
Better than before
Better than
Ever

We are a family
Perfectly formed
We are honest and open and ourselves
We are brave and strong and vulnerable and kind
We are together together together
We are made of love

## AN INTERVIEW BETWEEN MEG AND HER EDITOR

*Siobhán Parkinson is the author of more than thirty books and was the first ever Laureate na nÓg (Irish children's laureate). In 2010 she founded Little Island Books. Here Siobhán talks to Meg Grehan about* The Lonely Book.

**Meg, *The Lonely Book* is not just about a book — it's actually set in a bookshop. Which reminds me that the main character in your first book, *The Space Between*, worked in a bookshop. So it seems that you are drawn to bookshops as rather enchanting places. Have you ever worked in a bookshop, or is it just a dream?**
I love bookshops. When I found it harder to leave my house they were real sanctuaries to me, little homes away from my real home. If I could get home I was OK, and if I could get to a bookshop I was OK. I think bookshops are so special, so unlike anywhere else.

I did work in a bookshop! I was a bookseller and I did most of the ordering. I loved getting to talk to people about books, help them with their most specific and niche requests. *I need a book about a sloth, I need a book about the high seas, I need a book about ...* I loved that! Getting to know people has always been easiest for me when it's through books. I feel confident that I know and understand the world of books and it's where I feel safest, so working in a bookshop was very special to me.

**In this story, the bookshop has a very special kind of magic. It is the bookshop itself that chooses certain books and makes sure that they find their ideal readers. Later in the story, when one unattached book doesn't find its person, the bookshop gets very agitated. How did you come up with such an extraordinary device?**

When I worked in the bookshop I had a little desk down the back where I would unbox all the new books I'd ordered. There were a few instances when someone would come up and say, 'Oh, I heard about this book, it's about ...' and I would have that very book sitting right in front of me! They always reacted like it was magic, and I always kind of felt like it was.

**Annie is not exactly the main character (that is probably Charlie); but Annie is a main charac-ter in another sense, because the story is told**

from her point of view. That was an interesting decision. What made you think of telling it that way?

I agree that Charlie is really the main character, but for this book Annie made sense as the character whose point of view we follow. In *The Deepest Breath*, we followed Stevie as she discovered that she liked girls. It made sense to follow Stevie on that journey, as she was starting from the beginning. It's the same with Annie: she doesn't know anything about gender at the start of the story and it makes her the perfect character to learn and grow with. Just like with *The Deepest Breath*, I wanted to introduce concepts gently and carefully and in a positive way, and following Annie allowed me to do that.

I suppose Annie's openness to new ideas is something that comes naturally to her, as a child – when you are small, everything is new, and you haven't acquired too many prejudices. So that makes her an ideal narrator, would you agree?

I do agree! It's what's so amazing about children, isn't it? They learn and learn and learn every day, they are so open and ready for new things and so, so brave.

I wrote *The Deepest Breath* and *The Lonely Book* for younger readers because they both deal with topics I don't think are written about enough for children. Queer stories are for everyone, and I wanted to share some!

**Annie suffers from anxiety and she finds sometimes she can't speak. Can you tell us a bit about selective mutism and why you chose to explore it in this story?**

Selective mutism is a type of anxiety disorder that means that sometimes you just can't speak. I decided to write about it because I have it. In times of extreme stress I lose the ability to speak. For instance, during the height of the pandemic I couldn't speak at all for almost a year. My speech slowly came back but it was quite scary. Generally it just manifests in little ways: like, in an argument, sometimes words just vanish for me. It feels like quite a betrayal because I have always considered words friends. Writing about it, however minor a subplot it may be, was really nice for me. It reminded me that words take many forms and I am never truly without them.

**Using sign language to overcome mutism is a creative as well as a very loving response, and the whole family becomes involved. Can you tell us a bit about that?**

Again, that comes from personal experience. For those months when I couldn't speak my girlfriend and I learned sign language. We learned together and it was a very beautiful thing. It was her idea. We loved learning it, we loved using it and I loved it so much that she learned it with me; and that made me feel so loved and respected and valued. And so that is why I wrote that into the story of *The Lonely Book*. It just seemed right.

**The love that Annie and Charlie share with their mothers is very strong, very warm, very sustaining, and emotionally very satisfying to read about. But I like how you don't allow the fact that this family is united in love and togetherness to be an easy solution to their anxieties. Can you tell us a bit more about your thinking on this?**

I am very lucky to be in a relationship for almost twelve years now with a warm, funny, kind and caring person. I am loved and cared for and supported beyond what I ever thought possible. But I still have my anxieties, my troubles, my worries and struggles. The love I receive and the love I give can soothe these worries, they can lessen the load, they can calm me when things get too much. But they cannot take them away.

It isn't fair to expect a person, no matter who they are, to fix your problems or take away your struggles with just the power of love and togetherness. But it is OK to expect respect and love and tenderness, I think. That's what this family do: they love and respect and care for each other because they are a family and this is what comes naturally to them. They don't expect to fix everything for each other.

This is what Annie is learning: you can't fix everything for a person, even if you wish you could. But you can love them and support them and be there for them, and that can be just as powerful.

**All your books, Meg, are verse novels. Do you find that verse comes to you more naturally than prose?**

It definitely comes more naturally to me. I have always, always loved poetry. My nana wrote poetry and she wrote a poem about me when I was little. I still have the book that it's published in on my bookcase. I like to think she wrote me into the world of poetry.

**What a gift!**

Wasn't it just?

I was also a drama kid. I performed poetry I loved and wrote and performed my own poetry. I've always read it, always written it, and always loved it. So when I learned that I could write a whole story in a poetic form, a new world opened up to me. It just comes naturally to me, it makes me happy, it makes me feel free and brave and inspired.

I try quite hard to make my verse accessible and make it flow nicely so it isn't too taxing to read and I hope that readers feel that. I think people are often surprised by how much they like verse, and that kind of delights me!

**Thank you, Meg, for talking to me, and thank you for this wonderful book.**

# ACKNOWLEDGEMENTS

I don't usually write acknowledgements. Mostly because I'm worried I won't do it right or, god forbid, I'll forget someone. But this is a special book to me, written during a particularly trying time, so I really need to thank some very lovely people.

Thank you
    To my family, especially my mum, my brothers (including you, Daire), Lu and Paul. Your love means everything to me, you are beautiful, funny, smart, kind and wonderful people, all of you, and it is a true gift to know you, to love you and to have you in my life.

Thank you
    To my nana, for writing me right into the world of words and poems. I love you, I miss you, I understand you.

Thank you
    To everyone at Little Island. Matthew, Siobhan, Elizabeth and Kate. I really feel I found a beautiful little home with you. Thank you for your kindness, patience and guidance. I feel safe, seen and heard with Little Island, and I appreciate that more than I can say. Thank you for giving my books a home, for lifting my voice and understanding and supporting me and my characters so beautifully.

Thank you

To Nene, for the dreamiest cover I could ever hope for. I feel very undeserving of your talent but am endlessly thankful for it!

Thank you

To Courtney, for your friendship and encouragement. For making me smile whenever my phone lights up.

Thank you

To Rob, for your endless support, your loyalty and for being such a beautiful, grounding presence in my life. Let's sprint soon!

Thank you

To ci to ci to ci

Thank you

To anyone who has ever read any of my books. To anyone who has messaged me about them, posted about them or quietly appreciated them. Thank you for reminding me why I write. Thank you for welcoming my characters into your lives. Thank you for sharing these stories with me. They are not mine. They are ours.

**ALSO BY MEG GREHAN**

For readers age 10+

## *The Deepest Breath*

There is so much that Stevie doesn't know. She doesn't know about all the fish in the sea. She doesn't know all the constellations of the stars. And she doesn't know why she feels this way about Chloe.

Winner: Judges' Special Prize, KPMG Children's Books Ireland Awards 2020

For readers age 13+

## *The Space Between*

It's New Year's Eve, and Beth plans to spend a whole year alone, in her snug, safe house. But she has reckoned without floppy-eared, tail-wagging Mouse, who comes nosing to her window. Followed shortly by his owner, Alice.

Winner: Éilís Dillon Award, Children's Books Ireland Awards 2018

For readers age 13+

## *Baby Teeth*

Immy has been in love before – many times, across many lifetimes. But never as deeply, as intensely as this. Claudia has never been in love like this either. But then, this is her first time with a vampire.

A *Kirkus* Best YA Book of the Year 2022

## ABOUT MEG GREHAN

Meg Grehan is originally from County Louth but now hiding away in County Donegal in the north-west of Ireland, with a very ginger girlfriend, an even more ginger dog and an undisclosed number of cats (none of whom is ginger). Her first book *The Space Between* won the Éilís Dillon Award at the 2018 Children's Books Ireland Awards. *The Deepest Breath* won the Judge's Special Prize at the 2020 Children's Books Ireland Awards and was shortlisted for the Waterstones Children's Book Prize. It is published in the USA by Houghton Mifflin Harcourt and in France by Talents Haut. *Baby Teeth* was a *Kirkus* Best YA Book of 2022 and was nominated for the 2023 Carnegie Medal.

# ABOUT LITTLE ISLAND

Little Island is an independent Irish press that publishes the best writing for young readers. Founded in 2010 by Ireland's first children's laureate, Siobhán Parkinson, Little Island books are found throughout Ireland, the UK and North America, and have been translated into many languages around the world.

## RECENT AWARDS FOR LITTLE ISLAND BOOKS

**Spark! School Book Awards 2022: Fiction ages 9+**
*Wolfstongue* by Sam Thompson

**Book of the Year**
**KPMG Children's Books Ireland Awards 2021**
*Savage Her Reply* by Deirdre Sullivan

**YA Book of the Year**
**Literacy Association of Ireland Awards 2021**
*Savage Her Reply* by Deirdre Sullivan

**YA Book of the Year**
**An Post Irish Book Awards 2020**
*Savage Her Reply* by Deirdre Sullivan

**White Raven Award 2021**
*The Gone Book* by Helena Close

**Judges' Special Prize**
**KPMG Children's Books Ireland Awards 2020**
*The Deepest Breath* by Meg Grehan